THE HAUNTED CHAMBER

BY

ANN RADCLIFFE

Copyright © 2013 Read Books Ltd.
This book is copyright and may not be
reproduced or copied in any way without
the express permission of the publisher in writing

British Library Cataloguing-in-Publication Data
A catalogue record for this book is available from the
British Library

CONTENTS

ANN RADCLIFFE 1

THE HAUNTED CHAMBER 3

THE PROVENÇAL TALE... 16

ANN RADCLIFFE

Ann Radcliffe was born in Holborn, London in 1764. Very little is known about her early life – as *The Edinburgh Review* stated in her obituary, " 'she never appeared in public, nor mingled in private society, but kept herself apart, like the sweet bird that sings its solitary notes, shrouded and unseen." What is known is that in 1787, she married Oxford graduate and journalist William Radcliffe. He often returned home late, and to occupy her time she began to write and read her work to him when he returned home. Over the course of her life, Radcliffe would go on to publish a total of six novels. Her style was romantic, marked by vivid descriptions of landscapes, and yet it contains a strong supernatural streak which makes Radcliffe a founder and pioneer of Gothic literature. She was hugely popular during her lifetimes, and to this day her novel *The Mysteries of Udolpho* is an essential Gothic text (as, to a lesser degree, is *The Italian)*. She died in 1823, apparently from an asthma attack.

THE HAUNTED CHAMBER

THE count gave orders for the north apartments to be opened and prepared for the reception of Ludovico; but Dorothee, remembering what she had lately witnessed there, feared to obey; and not one of the other servants daring to venture thither, the rooms remained shut up till the time when Ludovico was to retire thither for the night, an hour for which the whole household waited with the greatest impatience.

After supper, Ludovico, by the order of the count, attended him in his closet, where they remained alone for near half an hour, and on leaving which his lord delivered to him a sword.

'It has seen service in mortal quarrels,' said the count, jocosely; 'you will use it honourably no doubt in a spiritual one. Tomorrow let me hear that there is not one ghost remaining in the château.'

Ludovico received it with a respectful bow. 'You shall be obeyed, my lord,' said he; 'I will engage that no spectre shall disturb the peace of the château after this night.'

They now returned to the supper-room, where the count's

guests awaited to accompany him and Ludovico to the north apartments; and Dorothee, being summoned for the keys, delivered them to Ludovico, who then led the way, followed by most of the inhabitants of the château. Having reached the back staircase, several of the servants shrunk back and refused to go further, but the rest followed him to the top of the staircase, where a broad landing-place allowed them to flock round him, while he applied the key to the door, during which they watched him with as much eager curiosity as if he had been performing some magical rite.

Ludovico, unaccustomed to the lock, could not turn it, and Dorothee, who had lingered far behind, was called forward, under whose hand the door opened slowly, and her eye glancing within the dusky chamber, she uttered a sudden shriek and retreated. At this signal of alarm the greater part of the crowd hurried down, and the count, Henri, and Ludovico were left alone to pursue the inquiry, who instantly rushed into the apartment, Ludovico with a drawn sword, which he had just time to draw from the scabbard, the count with a lamp in his hand, and Henri carrying a basket containing provision for the courageous adventurer.

Having looked hastily round the first room, where nothing appeared to justify alarm, they passed on to the second; and here too all being quiet, they proceeded to a third in a more tempered step. The count had now leisure to smile at the discomposure into which he had been surprised, and to ask Ludovico in which room he designed to pass the night.

'There are several chambers beyond these, your excellenza,' said Ludovico, pointing to a door, 'and in one of them is a bed, they say. I will pass the night there; and when I am weary of watching, I can lie down.'

'Good,' said the count; 'let us go on. You see, these rooms show nothing but damp walls and decaying furniture. I have been so much occupied since I came to the château, that I have not looked into them till now. Remember, Ludovico, to tell the housekeeper tomorrow to throw open these windows. The damask hangings are dropping to pieces; I will have them taken down, and this antique furniture removed.'

'Dear sir,' said Henri, 'here is an armchair so massy with gilding, that it resembles one of the state chairs in the Louvre more than anything else.'

'Yes,' said the count, stopping a moment to survey it, 'there is a history belonging to that chair, but I have not time to tell it; let us pass on. This suite runs to a greater extent than I imagined; it is many years since I was in them. But where is the bedroom you speak of, Ludovico? These are only ante-chambers to the great drawing-room. I remember them in their splendour.'

'The bed, my lord,' replied Ludovico, 'they told me was in a room that opens beyond the saloon and terminates the suite.'

'O, here is the saloon,' said the count, as they entered the spacious apartment in which Emily and Dorothee had rested. He here stood for a moment, surveying the reliques of faded grandeur which it exhibited, the sumptuous tapestry, the long and low sofas of velvet with frames heavily carved and gilded, the floor inlaid with small squares of fine marble, and covered in the centre with a piece of rich tapestry work, the casements of painted glass, and the large Venetian mirrors of a size and quality such as that period France could not make, which reflected on every side the spacious apartment. These had also formerly reflected a gay and brilliant scene, for this had been the state room of the château, and here the marchioness had held the assemblies that made part of the festivities of her nuptials. If the wand of a magician could have recalled the vanished groups – many of them vanished even from the earth! – that once had passed over these polished mirrors, what a varied and contrasted picture would they have exhibited with the present! Now, instead of a blaze of lights, and a splendid and busy crowd, they reflected only the rays of the one glimmering lamp which the count held up, and which scarcely served to show the three forlorn figures that stood surveying the room, and the spacious and dusky walls around them.

'Ah!' said the count to Henri, awaking from his deep

reverie, 'how the scene is changed since last I saw it! I was a young man then, and the marchioness was alive and in her bloom; many other persons were here too, who are now no more. There stood the orchestra, here we tripped in many a sprightly maze – the walls echoing to the dance. Now they resound only one feeble voice, and even that will, ere long, be heard no more. My son, remember that I was once as young as yourself, and that you must pass away like those who have preceded you – like those who, as they sung and danced in this most gay apartment, forgot that years are made up of moments, and that every step they took carried them nearer to their graves. But such reflections are useless – I had almost said criminal – unless they teach us to prepare for eternity, since otherwise they cloud our present happiness without guiding us to a future one. But enough of this – let us go on.'

Ludovico now opened the door of the bedroom, and the count, as he entered, was struck with the funeral appearance which the dark arras gave to it. He approached the bed with an emotion of solemnity, and, perceiving it to be covered with a pall of black velvet, paused. 'What can this mean?' said he, as he gazed upon it.

'I have heard, my lord,' said Ludovico, as he stood at the feet, looking within the canopied curtains, 'that the Lady Marchioness de Villeroi died in this chamber, and remained here till she was removed to be buried; and this perhaps, signor, may account for the pall.'

The count made no reply, but stood for a few moments engaged in thought, and evidently much affected. Then, turning to Ludovico, he asked him with a serious air, whether he thought his courage would support him through the night. 'If you doubt this,' added the count, 'do not be ashamed to own it; I will release you from your engagement without exposing you to the triumphs of your fellow-servants.' Ludovico paused; pride and something very like fear seemed struggling in his breast: pride, however, was victorious; – he blushed, and his hesitation ceased.

'No, my lord,' said he, 'I will go through with what I have begun; and I am grateful for your consideration. On that hearth I will make a fire; and with the good cheer in this basket, I doubt not I shall do well.'

'Be it so,' said the count: 'but how will you beguile the tediousness of the night, if you do not sleep?'

'When I am weary, my lord,' replied Ludovico, 'I shall not fear to sleep; in the meanwhile, I have a book that will entertain me.'

'Well,' said the count, 'I hope nothing will disturb you; but if you should be seriously alarmed in the night, come to my apartment. I have too much confidence in your good sense and courage to believe you will be alarmed on slight grounds, or suffer the gloom of this chamber, or its remote situation, to overcome you with ideal terrors. Tomorrow I shall have to thank you for an important service; these rooms shall then be thrown open, and my people will then be convinced of their error. Good night, Ludovico; let me see you early in the morning, and remember what I lately said to you.'

'I will, my lord. Good night to your excellenza – let me attend you with the light.'

He lighted the count and Henri through the chambers to the outer door. On the landing-place stood a lamp, which one of the affrighted servants had left; and Henri, as he took it up, again bade Ludovico 'good night', who, having respectfully returned the wish, closed the door upon them and fastened it. Then, as he retired to the bedchamber, he examined the rooms through which he passed with more minuteness than he had done before; for he apprehended that some person might have concealed himself in them for the purpose of frightening him. No one, however, but himself was in these chambers; and leaving open the doors through which he passed, he came again to the great drawing-room, whose spaciousness and silent gloom somewhat startled him. For a moment he stood looking back through the long suite of rooms he had just quitted; and as he turned, perceiving a light and his own figure reflected in one of the large mirrors, he started. Other objects, too, were seen obscurely on its dark surface, but he paused not to examine them, and returned hastily into the bedroom, as he surveyed which, he observed the door of the Oriel, and opened it. All within was still. On looking round, his eye was caught by the portrait of the deceased marchioness, upon which he gazed for a considerable time with great attention and some surprise; and then, having examined the closet, he returned into the bedroom, where he kindled a wood fire, the bright blaze of which revived his spirit which had begun to yield to the gloom and silence of the place; for gusts of wind alone broke at intervals this silence. He now drew a small table and a chair near the fire, took a bottle of wine and some cold provision out of his basket, and regaled himself. When he had finished his repast he laid his sword upon the table, and not feeling disposed to sleep, drew from his pocket the book he had spoken of. It was a volume of old Provençal tales. Having stirred the fire into a brighter blaze, trimmed his lamp, and drawn his chair upon the hearth, he began to read; and his attention was soon wholly occupied by the scenes which the page disclosed.

The count, meanwhile, had returned to the supper-room, whither those of the party who had attended him to the north apartment had retreated upon hearing Dorothee's scream, and who were now earnest in their inquiries concerning those chambers. The count rallied his guests on their precipitate retreat, and on the superstitious inclinations which had occasioned it; and this led to the question, whether the spirit, after it has quitted the body, is ever permitted to revisit the earth; and if it is, whether it was possible for spirits to become visible to the sense? The baron was of opinion, that the first was probable, and the last was possible; and he endeavoured to justify this opinion by respectable authorities, both ancient and modern, which he quoted. The count, however, was decidedly against him; and a long conversation ensued, in which the usual arguments on these subjects were on both sides brought forward with skill and discussed with candour, but without converting either party to the opinion of his opponent. The effect of their conversation on their auditors was various. Though the count had much the superiority of the baron in point of argument, he had fewer adherents; for that love, so natural to the human mind, of whatever is able to distend its faculties with wonder and astonishment, attached the majority of the company to the side of the baron; and though many of the count's propositions were unanswerable, his opponents were inclined to believe this the consequence of their own want of knowledge on so abstracted a subject, rather than that arguments did not exist which were forcible enough to conquer him.

Blanche was pale with attention, till the ridicule in her father's glance called a blush upon her countenance, and she then endeavoured to forget the superstitious tales she had been told in the convent. Meanwhile, Emily had been listening with deep attention to the discussion of what was to her a very interesting question; and remembering the appearance she had seen in the apartment of the late marchioness, she was frequently chilled with awe. Several times she was on the point of mentioning what she had seen, but the fear of giving pain to the count, and the dread of his ridicule, restrained her; and awaiting in anxious expectation the event of Ludovico's intrepidity, she determined that her future silence should depend upon it.

When the party had separated for the night, and the count retired to his dressing-room, the remembrance of the desolate scenes he had so lately witnessed in his own mansion deeply affected him, but at length he was aroused from his reverie and his silence. 'What music is that I hear?' said he suddenly to his valet. 'Who plays at this late hour?'

The man made no reply; and the count continued to listen, and then added, 'That is no common musician; he touches the instrument with a delicate hand. Who is it, Pierre?'

'My lord!' said the man, hesitatingly.

'Who plays that instrument?' repeated the count.

'Does not your lordship know, then?' said the valet.

'What mean you?' said the count, somewhat sternly.

'Nothing, my lord, I mean nothing,' rejoined the man submissively; 'only – that music – goes about the house at midnight often, and I thought your lordship might have heard it before.'

'Music goes about the house at midnight! Poor fellow! Does nobody dance to the music, too?'

'It is not in the château, I believe, my lord. The sounds come from the woods, they say, though they seem so very near; but then a spirit can do anything.'

'Ah, poor fellow!' said the count, 'I perceive you are as silly as the rest of them; tomorrow you will be convinced of your ridiculous error. But, hark! what noise is that?'

'Oh, my lord! that is the voice we often hear with music.'

'Often! said the count; 'how often, pray? It is a very fine one.'

'Why, my lord, I myself have not heard it more than two or three times; but there are those who have lived here longer, that have heard it often enough.'

'What a swell was that!' exclaimed the count, as he still listened; 'and now, what a dying cadence I This is surely something more than mortal.'

'That is what they say, my lord,' said the valet; 'they say it is nothing mortal that utters it; and if I might say my thoughts—'

'Peace!' said the count; and he listened till the strain died away.

'This is strange,' said he, as he returned from the window. 'Close the casements, Pierre.'

Pierre obeyed, and the count soon after dismissed him, but did not so soon lose the remembrance of the music, which long vibrated in his fancy in tones of melting sweetness, while surprise and perplexity engaged his thoughts.

Ludovico, meanwhile, in his remote chamber, heard now and then the faint echo of a closing door as the family retired to rest; and then the hall-clock, at a great distance, struck twelve. 'It is midnight,' said he, and he looked suspiciously round the spacious chamber. The fire on the hearth was now nearly expiring, for his attention having been engaged by the book before him, he had forgotten everything besides; but he soon added fresh wood, not because he was cold, though the night was stormy, but because he was cheerless; and having again trimmed the lamp, he poured out a glass of wine, drew his chair nearer to the crackling blaze, tried to be deaf to the wind that howled mournfully at the casements, endeavoured to abstract his mind from the melancholy that was stealing upon him, and again took up his book. It had been lent to him by Dorothee, who had formerly picked it up in an obscure corner of the marquis's library; and who, having opened it, and perceived some of the marvels it related, had carefully preserved it for her own entertainment, its condition giving her some excuse for detaining it from its proper station. The damp corner into which it had fallen, had caused the cover to be so disfigured and mouldy, and the leaves to be so discoloured with spots, that it was not without difficulty the letters could be traced. The fictions of the Provençal writers, whether drawn fom the Arabian legends brought by the Saracens into Spain, or recounting the chivalric exploits performed by crusaders whom the troubadours accompanied to the East, were generally splendid, and always marvellous both in scenery and incident; and it is not wonderful that Dorothee and Ludovico should be fascinated by inventions which had captivated the careless imagination in every rank of society in a former age. Some of the tales, however, in the book now before Ludovico were of simple structure, and exhibited nothing of the magnificent machinery and heroic manners which usually characterized the fables of the twelfth century, and of this description was the one he now happened to open; which in its original style was of great length, but may be thus shortly related. The reader will perceive it is strongly tinctured with the superstition of the times.

THE PROVENÇAL TALE

There lived, in the province of Bretagne, a noble baron, famous for his magnificence and courtly hospitalities. His castle was graced with ladies of exquisite beauty, and thronged with illustrious knights; for the honour he paid to feats of chivalry invited the brave of distant countries to enter his lists, and his court was more splendid than those of many princes. Eight minstrels were retained in his service, who used to sing to their harps romantic fictions taken from the Arabians, or adventures of chivalry that befell knights during the crusades, or the martial deeds of the baron, their lord; while he, surrounded by his knights and ladies, banqueted in the great hall of the castle, where the costly tapestry that adorned the walls with pictured exploits of his ancestors, the casements of painted glass enriched with armorial bearings, the gorgeous banners that waved along the roof, the sumptuous canopies, the profusion of gold and silver that glittered on the sideboards, the numerous dishes that covered the tables, the number and gay liveries of the attendants, with the chivalric and splendid attire of the guests, united to form a scene of magnificence such as we may not hope to see in these degenerate days.

Of the baron the following adventure is related: – One night, having retired late from the banquet to his chamber, and dismissed his attendants, he was surprised by the appearance of a stranger of a noble air, but of a sorrowful and dejected countenance. Believing that this person had been secreted in the apartment, since it appeared impossible he could have lately passed the ante-room unobserved by the pages in waiting, who would have prevented this intrusion on their lord, the baron, calling loudly for his people, drew his sword, which he had not yet taken from his side, and stood upon his defence. The stranger, slowly advancing, told him that there was nothing to fear; that he came with no hostile intent, but to communicate to him a terrible secret, which it was necessary for him to know.

The baron, appeased by the courteous manner of the stranger, after surveying him for some time in silence, returned his sword into the scabbard, and desired him to explain the means by which he had obtained access to the chamber, and the purpose of this extraordinary visit.

Without answering either of these inquiries, the stranger said that he could not then explain himself, but that, if the baron would follow him to the edge of the forest, at a short distance from the castle walls, he would there convince him that he had something of importance to disclose.

This proposal again alarmed the baron, who would scarcely believe that the stranger meant to draw him to so solitary a spot at this hour of the night without harbouring a design against his life, and he refused to go; observing at the same time, that if the stranger's purpose was an honourable one, he would not persist in refusing to reveal the occasion of his visit in the apartment where they stood.

While he spoke this, he viewed the stranger still more attentively than before, but observed no change in his countenance, nor any symptom that might intimate a consciousness of evil design. He was habited like a knight, was of a tall and majestic stature, and of dignified and courteous manners. Still, however, he refused to communicate the substance of his errand in any place but that he had mentioned; and at the same time gave hints concerning the secret he would disclose, that awakened a degree of solemn curiosity in the baron, which at length induced him to consent to the stranger on certain conditions.

'Sir knight,' said he, 'I will attend you to the forest, and will take with me only four of my people, who shall witness our conference.'

To this, however, the knight objected.

'What I would disclose,' said he with solemnity, 'is to you alone. There are only three living persons to whom the circumstance is known: it is of more consequence to you and your house than I shall now explain. In future years you will look back to this night with satisfaction or repentance, accordingly as you now determine. As you would hereafter prosper, follow me; I pledge you the honour of a knight that no evil shall befall you. If you are contented to dare futurity, remain in your chamber, and I will depart as I came.'

'Sir knight,' replied the baron; 'how is it possible that my future peace can depend upon my present determination?'

'That is not now to be told,' said the stranger; 'I have explained myself to the utmost. It is late: if you follow me it must be quickly; you will do well to consider the alternative.'

The baron mused, and, as he looked upon the knight, he perceived his countenance assume a singular solemnity.

(Here Ludovico thought he heard a noise, and he threw a glance round the chamber, and then held up the lamp to assist his observation; but not perceiving anything to confirm his alarm, he took up the book again, and pursued the story.)

The baron paced his apartment for some time in silence, impressed by the words of the stranger, whose extraordinary request he feared to grant, and feared also to refuse. At length he said, 'Sir knight, you are utterly unknown to me; tell me, yourself, is it reasonable that I should trust myself alone with a stranger, at this hour, in the solitary forest? Tell me, at least, who you are, and who assisted to secrete you in this chamber.'

The knight frowned at these words, and was a moment

silent; then, with a countenance somewhat stern, he said, 'I am an English knight; I am called Sir Bevys of Lancaster, and my deeds are not unknown at the holy city, whence I was returning to my native land, when I was benighted in the forest.'

'You name is not unknown to fame,' said the baron; 'I have heard of it.' (The knight looked haughtily.) 'But why, since my castle is known to entertain all true knights, did not your herald announce you? Why did you not appear at the banquet, where your presence would have been welcomed, instead of hiding yourself in my castle, and stealing to my chamber at midnight?'

The stranger frowned, and turned away in silence; but the baron repeated the questions.

'I come not,' said the knight, 'to answer inquiries, but to reveal facts. If you would know more, follow me; and again I pledge the honour of a knight that you shall return in safety. Be quick in your determination – I must be gone.'

After some farther hesitation, the baron determined to follow the stranger, and to see the result of his extraordinary request; he therefore again drew forth his sword, and, taking up a lamp, bade the knight lead on. The latter obeyed; and opening the door of the chamber, they passed into the ante-room, where the baron, surprised to find all his pages asleep, stopped, and with hasty violence was going to reprimand them for their carelessness, when the knight waved his hand, and looked so expressively at the baron, that the latter restrained his resentment, and passed on.

The knight, having descended a staircase, opened a secret door, which the baron had believed was only known to himself; and proceeding through several narrow and winding passages, came at length to a small gate that opened beyond the walls of the castle. Perceiving that these secret passages were so well known to a stranger, the baron felt inclined to turn back from an adventure that appeared to partake of treachery as well as danger. Then, considering that he was armed, and observing the courteous and noble air of his conductor, his courage returned, he blushed that it had failed him for a moment, and he resolved to trace the mystery to its source.

He now found himself on the healthy platform, before the great gates of his castle, where, on looking up, he perceived lights glimmering in the different casements of the guests, who were retiring to sleep; and while he shivered in the blast, and looked on the dark and desolate scene around him, he thought of the comforts of his warm chamber, rendered cheerful by the blaze of wood, and felt, for a moment, the full contrast of his present situation.

(Here Ludovico paused a moment, and, looking at his own fire, gave it a brightening stir.)

The wind was strong, and the baron watched his lamp with anxiety, expecting every moment, to see it extinguished; but though the flame wavered, it did not expire, and he still followed the stranger, who often sighed as he went, but did not speak.

When they reached the borders of the forest, the knight turned and raised his head, as if he meant to address the baron, but then closing his lips, in silence he walked on.

As they entered beneath the dark and spreading boughs, the baron, affected by the solemnity of the scene, hesitated whether to proceed, and demanded how much farther they were to go. The knight replied only by a gesture, and the baron, with hesitating steps and a suspicious eye, followed through an obscure and intricate path, till, having proceeded a considerable way, he again demanded whither they were going, and refused to proceed unless he was informed.

As he said this, he looked at his own sword and at the knight alternately, who shook his head, and whose dejected countenance disarmed the baron, for a moment, of suspicion.

'A little farther is the place whither I would lead you,' said the stranger; 'no evil shall befall you – I have sworn it on the honour of a knight.'

The baron, reassured, again followed in silence, and they soon arrived at a deep recess of the forest, where the dark and lofty chestnuts entirely excluded the sky, and which was so overgrown with underwood that they proceeded with difficulty. The knight sighed deeply as he passed, and sometimes paused; and having at length reached a spot where the trees crowded into a knot, he turned, and with a terrific look, pointing to the ground, the baron saw there the body of a man, stretched at its length, and weltering in blood; a ghastly wound was on the forehead, and death appeared already to have contracted the features.

The baron, on perceiving the spectacle, started in horror, looked at the knight for explanation, and was then going to raise the body, and examine if there were any remains of life; but the stranger, waving his hand, fixed upon him a look so earnest and mournful, as not only much surprised him, but made him desist.

But what were the baron's emotions when, on holding the lamp near the features of the corpse, he discovered the exact resemblance of the stranger his conductor, to whom he now looked up in astonishment and inquiry! As he gazed he perceived the countenance of the knight change and begin to fade, till his whole form gradually vanished from his astonished sense! While the baron stood, fixed to the spot, a voice was heard to utter these words:

(Ludovico started, and laid down the book for he thought he heard a voice in the chamber, and he looked towards the bed, where, however, he saw only the dark curtain and the pall. He listened, scarcely daring to draw his breath, but heard only the distant roaring of the sea in the storm, and the blast that rushed by the casements; when, concluding that he had been deceived by its sighings, he took up his book to finish his story.)

While the baron stood, fixed to the spot, a voice was heard to utter these words:

'The body of Sir Bevys of Lancaster, a noble knight of England, lies before you. He was this night waylaid and murdered, as he journeyed from the holy city towards his native land. Respect the honour of knighthood, and the law of humanity; inter the body in christian ground, and cause his murderers to be punished. As ye observe or neglect this, shall peace and happiness, or war and misery, light upon you and your house for ever!'

The baron, when he recovered from the awe and astonishment into which this adventure had thrown him, returned to his castle, whither he caused the body of Sir Bevys to be removed; and on the following day it was interred, with the honours of knighthood, in the chapel of the castle, attended by all the noble knights and ladies who graced the court of Baron de Brunne.

Ludovico, having finished this story, laid aside the book, for he felt drowsy; and after putting more wood on the

The Haunted Chamber

fire, and taking another glass of wine, he reposed himself in the armchair on the hearth. In his dream he still beheld the chamber where the rally was, and once or twice started from imperfect slumbers, imagining he saw a man's face looking over the high back of his armchair. This idea had so strongly impressed him, that, when he raised his eyes, he almost expected to meet other eyes fixed upon his own; and he quitted his seat, and looked behind the chair before he felt perfectly convinced that no person was there.

Thus closed the hour.

The count, who had slept little during the night, rose early, and, anxious to speak with Ludovico, went to the north apartment; but the outer door having been fastened on the preceding night, he was obliged to knock loudly for admittance. Neither the knocking nor his voice was heard: he renewed his calls more loudly than before; after which a total silence ensued; and the count, finding all his efforts to be heard ineffectual, at length began to fear that some accident had befallen Ludovico, whom terror of an imaginary being might have deprived of his senses. He therefore left the door with an intention of summoning his servants to force it open, some of whom he now heard moving in the lower part of the château.

To the count's inquiries whether they had seen or heard anything of Ludovico, they replied, in affright, that not one of them had ventured on the north side of the château since the preceding night.

'He sleeps soundly, then,' said the count, 'and is at such a distance from the outer door, which is fastened, that to gain admittance to the chambers it will be necessary to force it. Bring an instrument, and follow me.'

The servants stood mute and dejected, and it was not till nearly all the household were assembled, that the count's orders were obeyed. In the meantime, Dorothee was telling of a door that opened from a gallery leading from the great staircase into the last ante-room of the saloon, and this being much nearer to the bedchamber, it appeared probable that Ludovico might be easily awakened by an attempt to open it. Thither, therefore, the count went; but his voice was as ineffectual at this door as it had proved at the remoter one; and now, seriously interested for Ludovico, he was himself going to strike upon the door with the instrument, when he observed its singular beauty, and withheld the blow. It appeared on the first glance to be of ebony, so dark and close was its grain, and so high its polish; but it proved to be only of larch wood, of the growth of Provence, then famous for its forests of larch. The beauty of its polished hue, and of its delicate carvings, determined the count to spare this door, and he returned to that leading from the back staircase, which being at length forced, he entered the first ante-room, followed by Henri and a few of the most courageous of his servants, the rest waiting the event of the inquiry on the stairs and landing-place.

All was silence in the chambers through which the count passed, and, having reached the saloon, he called loudly upon Ludovico; after which, still receiving no answer, he threw open the door of the bedroom, and entered.

The profound stillness within confirmed his apprehensions for Ludovico, for not even the breathings of a person in sleep were heard; and his uncertainty was not soon terminated, since the shutters being all closed, the chamber was too dark for any object to be distinguished in it.

The count bade a servant open them, who, as he crossed the room to do so, stumbled over something, and fell to the floor, when his cry occasioned such a panic among the few of his fellows who had ventured thus far, that they instantly fled, and the count and Henri were left to finish the adventure.

Henri then sprang across the room, and, opening a window-shutter, they perceived that the man had fallen over a chair near the hearth, in which Ludovico had been sitting; – for he sat there no longer, nor could anywhere be seen by the imperfect light that was admitted into the apartment. The count, seriously alarmed, now opened other shutters, that he might be enabled to examine farther; and Ludovico not yet appearing, he stood for a moment suspended in astonishment, and scarcely trusting his senses, till his eyes glancing on the bed, he advanced to examine whether he was there asleep. No person, however, was in it; and he proceeded to the Oriel, where everything remained as on the preceding night; but Ludovico was nowhere to be found.

The count now checked his amazement, considering that Ludovico might have left the chambers during the night, overcome by the terrors which their lonely desolation and the recollected reports concerning them had inspired. Yet, if this had been the fact, the man would naturally have sought society, and his fellow-servants had all declared they had not seen him; the door of the outer room also had been found fastened, with the key on the inside; it was impossible, therefore, for him to have passed through that; and all the outer doors of this suite were found, on examination, to be bolted and locked, with the keys also within them. The count, being then compelled to believe that the lad had escaped through the casements, next examined them; but such as opened wide enough to admit the body of a man were found to be carefully secured either by iron bars or by shutters, and no vestige appeared of any person having attempted to pass them; neither was it probable that Ludovico would have incurred the risk of breaking his neck by leaping from a window, when he might have walked safely through a door.

The count's amazement did not admit of words; but he returned once more to examine the bedroom, where was no appearance of disorder, except that occasioned by the late overthrow of the chair, near which had stood a small table; and on this Ludovico's sword, his lamp, the book he had been reading, and the remains of his flask of wine, still remained. At the foot of the table, too, was the basket, with some fragments of provision and wood.

Henri and the servant now uttered their astonishment without reserve, and though the count said little, there was a seriousness in his manner that expressed much. It appeared that Ludovico must have quitted these rooms by some concealed passage, for the count could not believe that any supernatural means had occasioned this event; yet, if there was any such passage, it seemed inexplicable why he should retreat through it; and it was equally surprising, that not even the smallest vestige should appear by which his progress could be traced. In the rooms, everything remained as much in order as if he had just walked out by the common way.

The count himself assisted in lifting the arras with which the bedchamber, saloon, and one of the ante-rooms were hung, that he might discover if any door had been concealed behind it; but after a laborious search, none was found; and he at length quitted the apartments, having secured the door of the last antechamber the key of which he took into

The Haunted Chamber

his own possession. He then gave orders that strict search should be made for Ludovico, not only in the château, but in the neighbourhood, and retiring with Henri to his closet, they remained there in conversation for a considerable time; and whatever was the subject of it, Henri from this hour lost much of his vivacity; and his manners were particularly grave and reserved, whenever the topic, which now agitated the count's family with wonder and alarm, was introduced.*

* The château had been inhabited before the count came into its possession. He was not aware that the apparently outward walls contained a series of passages and staircases, which led to unknown vaults underground, and, therefore, he never thought of looking for a door in those parts of the chamber which he supposed to be next to the air. In these was a communication with the room. The château (for we are not here in Udolpho) was on the sea-shore in Languedoc; its vaults had become the store-house of pirates, who did their best to keep up the supernatural delusions that hindered people from searching the premises; and these pirates had carried Ludovico away.

www.ingramcontent.com/pod-product-compliance
Ingram Content Group UK Ltd.
Pitfield, Milton Keynes, MK11 3LW, UK
UKHW041227200426
11947UKWH00034B/237